This edition published 2010 by Zero to Ten Ltd,
Part of the Evans Publishing Group,
2a Portman Mansions,
Chiltern Street,
London W1U 6NR

British Library Cataloguing in Publication Data
A CIP catalogue record for this book is available from the British Library

ISBN 9781840896343

Printed in China

Billy on the Ball

by Paul Harrison

illustrated by Silvia Raga

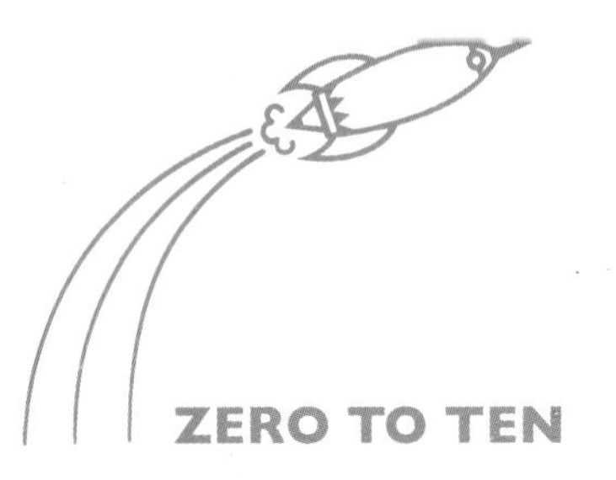

It's cup final day.

Billy's on the team.

The ground is full.

The game kicks off.

Billy heads the ball...

...and gets fouled.

Yellow card!

Billy's on the ball again.

He shoots,

he scores!

He's won the game!

He gets the trophy.

He lifts it high.

He wakes up!